T0354692

Other Books

Life is Good

A Tale of Discovery

Shelter in Place

A Case of Espionage

The Terrorist Plot

The Final Escape

Everything is Good

and

Advanced Lessons in Artificial Intelligence

THE MONEY GATE

A TIMELY NOVEL

HARRY KATZAN JR.

iUniverse

THE MONEY GATE
A TIMELY NOVEL

iUniverse books may be ordered through booksellers or by contacting:

iUniverse
1663 Liberty Drive
Bloomington, IN 47403
www.iuniverse.com
844-349-9409

ISBN: 978-1-6632-6711-5 (sc)
ISBN: 978-1-6632-6713-9 (hc)
ISBN: 978-1-6632-6712-2 (e)

Library of Congress Control Number: 2024920062

Print information available on the last page.

iUniverse rev. date: 09/20/2024

CONTENTS

INTRODUCTION

This is an adventure novel in the Matt, Ashley, and the General series This book is different than usual. This book is modern, up to date, and relevant to the modern world of everyday life. The book is a complete novel with characters, a location, and a context. It is a relevant story to everyday occurrences and modern values.

It is intended for full use as a reading book, but is designed to be a converted to a model for professional writer to use in a movie or play.

A freelance writer breaks the drama into scenes, persons, and events. This book assists in doing so. However, it is intended to be rewritten for the project in which it is to be used.

The book is written so that the story can easily be extended to match the point of view of the writer. They are professionals and know how to do it.

In this book, the story as it is published with no violence, no sex, and no bad language. However, the play or movie writer can change the characterization to meet his or her needs.

The text has a destination and it is headed for an election, as in the saga of the famous Watercate scandal. However, as you will read, it ends differently. This can be up to the professional writer.

The characters are likeable and real. There are numerous scenes that the professional writer can use to his or her advantage.

You will like the characters: Matt, Ashley, the General, General Clark, the President, and Bob and Margaret, who you will hear about.

The story is short and easy to read. You can enjoy it on a car, train, or airplane ride. The final chapter takes a quick look at the Watergate incident.

You can leave the author's version on the coffee table for everyone to see and comment on.

Please enjoy the novel.

The Author
September, 2024

MAIN CHARACTERS
IN THE STORY

The General – Les Miller. Former military General and Humanitarian. P-51 pilot and World War II hero.

Matthew (Matt) Miller – Professor of Mathematics. Grandson of the General. Sophisticated problem solver and strategist.

Ashley Wilson Miller – College friend of Matt Miller. Married to Matt Miller. Receiver of the National Medal of Freedom.

Marguerite Purgoine - Retired creative writing Professor and an associate of the team. Known as Anna for some unknown reason. Wife of the General.

General Clark – Mark Clark, Former Four Star General and Chairman of the Joint Chiefs of Staff, Appointed to be U.S. Director of Intelligence.

Kimberly Scott – The Intelligence specialist of the U.S. Has an extensive publications record.

Harry Steevens – Expert mathematician and former college friend of Matt Miller. Policeman in New Jersey.

Robert (Bob) Anderson – Retired Professor and associate of Matt Miller.

Margaret Anderson – Insightful wife of Bob Anderson.

PROLOGUE

The book involves a string of ladies, having lost their husbands, through various reasons or methods, entice live-in boyfriends to provide large sums of money to those ladies. The methods are varied and quite ingenuous.

The story begins when Matt is visited by a former university associate about an unusual occurrence he has experienced. Matt's academic friend, a retired professor of Mathematics, is concerned about the disappearance of his buddy from the breakfast club sponsored by their church.

This and other clever endeavors are distasteful in general, a discredit to the United States of America, and especially to the persons involved.

After a brief introduction to and description of the people in the story, the drama begins with the visit to Matt at is home.

CHAPTER 1

◆ ◆ ◆ ◆ ◆

ABOUT THE GENERAL

As mentioned in the introduction, the main characters in this story are the General, Matt, Bud and Ashley. Here is a snapshot of exactly who we are talking about when we refer to the General in the ensuing dialog. He is a retired three star general officer who achieved a rank of Lieutenant General in the U.S. Army. In civilian life he is referred to as *The General*, because of his record of accomplishment in and out of the military. He holds bachelors, masters, and doctorate degrees and is the founder of a prestigious political polling company. The following snapshot also includes Lt. Charles (Buzz) Bunday, the General's wing man, and the Air Force commander during World War II. In the following paragraph, the person called the General is Lt. Les Miller.

The following scene begins the General's scenario. The Air Force commander and Buzz Bunday are waiting for Lt. Les Miller to return from his bombing mission in the new U.S. fighter plane known as the P-51. As the saying goes, if you have a P-51 on your tail, you're a goner – that is, the enemy. The fighters normally accompany and protect bombers, such as the B-17 that are on a bombing mission against the enemy. In this instance, Miller is on the tail of a German fighter plane that shot down a U.S. B-17 bomber. Buzz radioed Miller to forget the enemy because he, Les Miller, might use up his fuel. Tired of waiting for Miller to return, the flight commander said, "He's either run out of fuel or got shot down." Buzz, who is

1

Miller 's buddy, replied, "Let's give him a few more minutes." The commander answered, "You've got 2 minutes Lieutenant. I've got work to do."

"I hear something," said Buzz. "It sounds like a 51. It's him." The commander replied, "His engine just shut off, must be he's out of fuel." Les Miller, the General, makes a dead stick landing and runs into a barrier, put up for that purpose. The General jumps out of his P-51 and says, "I got him, he's a goner. That is 36 kills for me." The commander turns and says that the two lieutenants should report to him in the morning at 8:00. The two pilots have completed the Air Force requirement of 25 missions and are quite proud of themselves, as most fighter pilots are shot down before they make the minimum requirement. All Miller says Is, "That Is why he Is a commander; that man has no feeling about other people."

In the commander's office at 8:00 the next morning, the pilots enter and salute the commander. "At ease gentlemen," says the commander. "By my records, you have completed your Air Force requirement of 25 flights. Attention! You are now promoted to the rank of Captain, U.S. Army Air Force, with all rights and privileges pertaining thereto. In your case Bunday, you have the British equivalent. Both of you have two weeks leave in the states and are then ordered to report to the Pentagon for duty or assignment. Your leave expenses are covered by the government. Good luck." That was the end of World War II combat for the General and Buzz.

The two pilots enjoyed their two weeks in New York City, along with a fine hotel and good food. Buzz, born and raised in England, is amazed by the quality of life in what many Englanders refer to as the colonies. As World War II servicemen, the men appreciate the famous Statue of Liberty given to the U.S. by France. They agree that it is quite impressive.

At the Pentagon, Captain Miller and Captain Bunday were ordered to report to a high level secret meeting concerning the number of P-51s shot down in a single mission, which is roughly 60%. The high command of the U.S. and Britain believe that a failure rate that high cannot be sustained in terms of personnel and equipment.

The Air Force tried titanium panels as armament and the method did not work. So, the big guns were brought in to solve the problem. The meeting is being attended by three-star generals, college professors, and noted scientists. They laugh when the Captains are introduced. "What good are a couple of Captains when the smartest men in the country cannot solve the problem." The problem is well defined. All of the bullet holes are covered up but the planes continue to be shot down. Captain Les Miller says, "I can solve the problem." The others just laughed and they took a coffee break. Buzz says, "Les, are you out of your mind? You're probably going to get us demoted."

Les replied, "Don't worry Buzz, I'll solve the problem."

"What did you major in in college?" asked Buzz.

"Math," said Captain Miller, "but as I said, don't worry about it."

"I certainly hope you are right," said Buzz.

When the meeting got going again, Captain Miller was asked to describe the method that he says will solve the problem. Here is Miller's response. "The objective of the meeting is to determine where titanium plates are to be placed for protection of P-51s. Here are some photos." The photos showed P-51s with bullet holes. "The planes have been plated where the holes are with no improvement. Now, that is the reason why we are here. It's an easy problem." The rest of the audience just laughed and looked at each other. One officer mentioned so everyone could hear him. "This guy is a joker. I thought that was why they were there, to help us solve the problem. The new Captain is off his rocker."

Captain Miller calmly continued, "It's easy gentlemen. The important holes went down with the plane – in fact, probably caused it. Look at the photos, do you see any planes with holes in the bellies, for example. We should plating areas where there is no holes."

The audience just looked at each other. That was the solution to their problem.

"If the Army Air Force armor would armor plate the untouched areas evident in the photos we have, the problem will be solved," said Miller.

The armor plating was placed in clean aircraft bellies, and the percent of shot down planes was reduced to 10%. Note, this is a true story. Captain Miller, and his buddy Bunday were promoted forthwith to the rank of Major. Again, this is a true story. The author has researched it and read the descriptive math paper that describes it. It was termed *reverse mathematics* for lack of a better name. A distinguished professor eventually worked on it for some time.

The General was and is an avid golfer, being a member of a local country club, at which he and his grandson Dr. Matt Miller play at least twice in a week. The General also established an upscale restaurant named the *Green Room*, that he used for business and pleasure.

The General owns a personal aircraft named the Gulfstream 650 that was purchased with personal money. A few years later, he obtained a small business jet for short trips. The General was an experienced military pilot having flown P-51s, B-17s, B-25s, and B-29s.. He never piloted his own personal aircraft.

The General's first wife died early on and he eventually married Dr. Marguerite Purgoine, a professor at a local prestigious university, and known by the moniker Anna, who was Matt and Ashley's writing instructor.

The General has numerous friends in the Army. One of which is General Mark Clark, four-star Chief of Staff, and eventually Director of Intelligence. The General is also the friend of the President and the First Lady.

CHAPTER 2
$\leftrightarrow\leftrightarrow\leftrightarrow\leftrightarrow$

MATT AND ASHLEY

Two students trudged up the three flights of stairs to the spacious apartment at 54 Nassau Street, the dwelling of Mme. Marguerite Purgoine, a professor of creative writing at the university. She was an internationally accredited prize-winning author who commanded the respect of the authorities in charge, whoever they were. Marguerite, called Anna for unknown reasons, was a sweet woman of questionable years. To the older professors, she was young. To the students, she was old. She was the only faculty member allowed to teach from her home, and the only faculty member having to climb up the terrible three flights of stairs. She was in good shape for her age.

The students were strangers. The boy initiated the conversation, "Hi, my name is Matthew Miller, but most people call me Matt. Are you going to make it?" The girl pleased that he broke the ice replied, "Well, I think so. I'm not so athletic. My mom wanted to be a soccer mom, and now I hate running and exercise of all kinds. My name is Ashley Wilson." The couple ploughed upward until they reached the apartment.

The door was open wide to a very large studio with enormous bookshelves and thousands of books scattered practically everywhere. A few students were already there seated in chairs placed in a semi-circle. The professor was a small gray haired aristocratic-looking lady who welcomed the newcomers with a "Welcome to creative writing." The latest couple grabbed the two vacant chairs and the teacher was ready to begin with the course. "Welcome to the most worthwhile course you are going to take at this prestigious university. My name is Marguerite Purgoine and I will be your teacher. In the class, and with email and messaging, I would prefer that you call me Anna – heaven only knows where that name came from – but on the street or campus, please call me Professor Purgoine or Dr. Purgoine. I want you to enjoy the course, because happy writers are good writers. I am well aware of grade inflation throughout the country and especially on this campus, so just do your job and I will take care of you. You probably already know where the phrase 'just do your job' comes from. In case you don't, it comes from the grand old game of football. When a player tries to gain favor with the coach asking what he should do better, they frequently get the reply, 'just do your job'. In your case, just do your job and turn in your writing assignments on time."

Matt smiled at Ashley and she smiled back.

Matt and Ashley became college friends, as a result of the college writing course, and met casually at Starbucks and the library. Matt was a college golf champion and Ashley was a practicing drama student. That means she was in some plays. Matt was a dedicated student who possessed an exceptional amount of common sense. Ashley was interested in becoming a noteworthy actress, eventually marrying an English Prince. Matt graduated with a PhD in math and started a successful academic career in the distinguished university from which he obtained his first degree. Ashley eventually became is well known actress and well know performer.

Ashley eventually married Matt. They were and are a good team. Ashley later became a professor of drama at a local college.

CHAPTER 3

THE BREAKFAST CLUB

The local church had a breakfast club for men, because after 30 years of working, and a dynamic go-go environment, it all came to an end when they retired. The club met the first and third Wednesdays of each month. Many of the men did not have much to do at home, and others were lonesome. In some cases, a man's spouse passed away and it was the only time in all their life that they were by themselves. Being lonesome is a terrible thing. The breakfast club was their only social event.

Bob Anderson, after many years of students, faculty, and university administration, has become adept in other's feelings and what to do about it. He knew the symptoms of a lonely person. Bob noticed a fellow who was friendly, well to do, and in need of a friend. At times, he looked as though he was about to cry. From Bob's view, he was lonely.

Bob struck up an acquaintance and his new found friend, named Alan Stockton, was extremely pleased. At first they played golf together and went to the driving range. But usually, they just talked. Alan had been an engineer in the space program and was accustomed to being extremely busy. Alan liked to help people, at first his mother and father, and then his wife and children. He needed to have someone to help, if only to go shopping with his wife. Alan's wife had recently passed away.

Alan consistently wanted to do expensive things, like taking a cruise or going down the river in a vacation area. Bob was much more reserved because he was careful about the family money. And he had an excellent home life.

Alan liked to tell stories and Bob was a good listener. When he wasn't in one of his lonesome moods, Alan was as happy as a lark and talked on and on. On most breakfast club Wednesday's, Bobby and Alan stayed on for a couple of cups of coffee.

They both liked to have a Carmel Macchiato and met frequently at the local Starbucks. Bob's wife Margaret did not mind, and she sometimes accompanied them. She didn't mind because she, like Bob, was that kind of person.

Then, all of a sudden, Alan seemed to be too busy for their usual activity. He missed a couple of Wednesday breakfasts and wasn't available for the driving range and the usual round of golf. Also, Alan took an expensive cruise. All Margaret said was, "Your friend Alan has a girl friend, and she runs the show. I'm glad to think that might be the case. He seems to be a real nice and thoughtful person. He needs companionship."

"I hope your are right," said Bob.

"I think I am," continued Margaret. "Didn't you mention that he previously took an ocean cruises and you must have mentioned Daisy to him. She goes on cruises."

"I almost forgot that both of us got haircuts from her," added Bob. "I did not know that Daisy went on cruises. She has that big house in which she has a one room hair operation. She must have plenty of money. I don't usually ask her too many questions, so she would not think I am interested in her. Is she married?"

"I don't think so," said Margaret. "She probably gets alimony and wants to keep it going. When I introduced her to you for a men's haircut, she always was nice to you. I suspect that she was also nice to Alan."

"I think she has a male companion," continued Margaret. "When I was at Walmart, I ran into her and started talking. We had just said a few words when this guy kind of pulled her off and said they were in a hurry and they just hurried off. He might live in. People do that now."

"Yeah," added Bob. "People do all kinds of things now."

"I wouldn't be too concerned about Alan," replied Margaret. "He'll come around when he wants someone to talk to or wants someone to have a Carmel Macchiato with him. He never came here. Did you ever see where he lived?"

"No, that subject never came up," answered Bob. "But come to think of it, when I left the last time, I went out through the front door and another guy, not Alan, was sitting at a bar of some kind and he was munching at a bag of potato chips. He simply nodded to me and I to him, I paid Daisy and was off out the door and gone."

CHAPTER 4

✦✦✦✦✦

BOB GETS A HAIRCUT FROM DAISY

Some time had passed and Bob was busy with a new found hobby, so to speak. He was writing a novel; something he always wanted to do. He had been bugging Margaret about it, and she finally said, "Write the novel, and I will type if for you. You never read a novel. How do you know what to write?"

"That's not exactly true," replied Bob. "I've read all of Agatha Christy's Heurot Poirot novels, all Conan Doyle novels, and also Daniel Silva's novels."

"When you wrote those math books, you had to write a preface and said you never had read one," replied Margaret. "Writing a novel will be good for your ego."

A few chapters of novel writing turned out to be harder to do than a math book. Bob and Margaret were going to attend a Fiddlers on the Roof play, and Margaret suggested that Bob would look better with a haircut. She said he looked like a writer. He concurred with a chuckle. So Margaret called Daisy and made an appointment for her husband.

Bob pushed the door bell, and Daisy said 'come in' and motioned for Bob to take a seat in the home hair dresser's salon, about the size of a mud room. Bob had just sat down when Daisy said, "He hit me."

All Bob said was, "I'm sorry to hear that. Are you okay?"

"And I had to pay him three hundred thousand dollars," continued Daisy.

"That's a lot," replied Bob. "Is that for his share of the house?"

Daisy nodded, and about that time the phone rang. From the conversation, Bob could tell it was about real estate. In the conversation, Daisy said forty-eight at one point.

Bob said using employing no diplomacy at all, "You must be 76 years old."

Daisy just looked at him with total surprise, and nodded. She liked Bob. He always surprised her. The haircut proceeded as usual and Daisy reverted to her usual talkative self. On the way out, there was no gentleman eating potato chips.

When Bob got home, Margaret was more than interested, and imagined about a dozen scenarios for Daisy's situation. Margaret surmised that Daisy had another boyfriend in addition to her live in one. Bob just said that the live-in boyfriend just had too much to drink, and Daisy got on his case.

As you probably imagined, three weeks later, Bob was back for another haircut. Daisy was very pleasant, as if nothing had happened a few weeks ago. In fact, Daisy went out to the garage for something and asked Bob to help her carry it in. In the corner of a massive garage, was a large container, probably to put the garden and lawn equipment. It was quite nice. Bob asked what it was for, and Daisy said that was where she stacked the bodies, and laughed. All Bob said was, "Now I know."

On the way out after the haircut, who was at the counter eating potato chips with a soft drink? Alan. The men cordially greeted each other and Bob left with a head full of questions.

CHAPTER 5

BOB AND MARGARET ANALYZE THE SITUATION

Bob got home and the first thing he said was, "Do I have the information. Let's go into the Living Room."

Margaret and Bob turned off the TV and sat down.

"What happened?" asked Margaret. "Are you okay?"

"Oh, I'm fine all right, but I really have the information," answered Bob.

"Was Daisy all right," asked Margaret.

"Daisy was fine," said Bob. "She was her cheerful self. Here's what happened. About half way through the haircut, she had to get something out of the garage, and she asked me to help her bring it in."

"What was it?" asked Margaret.

"It was some kind of equipment," said Bob. "But, when I was in the garage, I noticed the same large container at the other end. It was pretty high and had a door. It was nice. I thought it was for a lawn mower, or a tractor, or a motorcycle or something like that. It was unusual to me to have something like that in a garage. I again asked her what it was, and she said that was where she put the bodies. Then she laughed. She thought it was funny."

"What did you say?" replied Margaret.

"All I said was, ' Now I know.' What was I to say? It didn't seem funny to me."

"What else happened?" asked Margaret.

"She finished my haircut, and I paid her, and on the way out, you will never guess who was sitting at the counter eating potato chips and drinking a soft drink.," said Bob. "Alan."

"Alan, what was he doing there? As if I didn't know by now." said Margaret.

"I guess he was living there," answered Bob. "But the question is, 'Why did she say bodies? She could have said just about anything. But she specifically said 'bodies'."

"Maybe she was going to do something to the body of the first guy with the equipment you helped bring in," said Margaret. "Maybe Alan didn't know about it yet."

"Maybe the first guy didn't hit her, but she hit and killed him, and she did not have to pay three hundred thousand to him because he was already dead.," said Bob. " So now she owned the house all by herself then and could sell it for a large sum of money."

'Maybe the first guy paid her three hundred thousand and she just salted it away. And the first guy did not realize what was going on," said Margaret. "She could have a fake deed made up. And now she is going to have Alan give her another three hundred thousand to buy into the property, and the same thing is going to happen. What should we do?""""

"I don't know," said Bob. "I heard there is a professor at the University that gets into things like this for the government. His uncle or grandfather is a big shot in the government."

"Let's invite him over and after dinner and bring up the subject," said Margaret with a smile. She knew the person was Matt Miller, the guy with the beautiful movie-star wife, Ashley.

"Let me talk to him at the University and let you know," said Bob. "Maybe I can catch him this afternoon. "He always has his classes in the morning and is free afterwards."

Bob caught Matt, before he left for home, and Matt suggested that they meet at the Green Room. He asked if 6 o'clock would be okay and asked if could bring his grandfather, who owned the political polling company. He had been a General in the military. Matt also said to dress casually. Bob agreed and the date was set.

Matt got Ashley and headed out to talk to the General.

CHAPTER 6

✦✦✦✦✦

THE GREEN ROOM

Ashley was happy about the Green Room meeting; she loved to eat out and especially the Green Room. The General, on the other hand, was a bit skeptical. He thought there were better ways to spend their time and money. Ashley saved the day by mentioning that it might be related to the last project in which the President was concerned with what was happening right under his nose right in the White House. "There are a lot of spywork going on," she said. "And we should be aware of what the spies were after."

The General always liked Ashley, because she had a good head on her shoulders and frequently thought of things that flew over the heads of other people. The General agreed if he could bring along Anna, his professor/writer wife who once was Matt's and Ashley's college writing course professor. So all was said and done. Dinner at the Green Room at six.

───── ⊗⊗⊗ ─────

The General ordered a table out of the view of most diners, and ordered the maitre D' to give special attention to that table.

Matt and the General parked in front and waited for their guests to arrive. After a few minutes, the General asked the maitre D' if there were any stray guests in the restaurant, and the maitre D' said there were. They had been asking about a gentleman in an Army uniform. Matt walked over and asked them to come to the General's table. They all laughed, since Ashley made a joke about it. The General suggested they have dinner first and then adjoin to a small conference room in the rear of the restaurant. The men and the women got along splendidly. The General had single malt scotch, Matt and Bob had the new Budweiser Zero non-alcoholic beverage, and the ladies both had daquïris. The General suggested the beef filet and they all had loaded baked potatoes along with it. The General asked if they might enjoy English Treacle sponge pudding with caffeine free espresso in the conference room and they all agreed.

Anna stole the show with examples from the many writing courses she had at the college level. And of course, she had to mention Matt and Ashley, her favorite students and their writings that she had saved.

A lady and her husband watched the group with interest. The lady said, "They look splendidly along with their guests, even though they are dressed casually." Her husband replied, "Of course dear, they are Americans."

The table was set up in the conference room with water, paper and special liquid gel pens.

"Matt asked me to join you in investigating a strange situation wherein a woman with wealth ostensibly asks a gentleman to join with her in a living arrangement. The woman states that 'that he hit me" and removes him from her premises and gives him a large fee of three thousand dollars. So, how do we approach a situation like this?" said the General."

"I propose two simple case studies," continued the General. "In the first case, let's say they meet, supposedly fall in love, and began by living together is a modest residence. After a certain period of time, they agree to combine their individual wealth or part of it and live in a more wealthy home. Suppose the money is $300,000 each. They both have ownership. If something happens and the man moves out, the woman has to pay the man his contribution of $300,000, and she owns the property forthright. That is because she paid the original $300,000 and another $300,000 upon separation. They agree it could work out this way."

"In the second case, the woman owns the property outright right from the beginning and the man pays $300,000 to live with the woman. The woman's property is worth $600,000 and she receives the man's $300,000. It is not clear if his name is on the property deed. Upon separation, she says she has to pay him his $300,000. In one instance, she gives him the $300,000 and everything appears to be worked out. In the second instance, she does not pay him the $300,000 and disposes of him in some manner. Perhaps, he is alone in the world and nobody knows about it. In this case, she is clearly ahead $300,000."

"And then she does it again, and again, and so forth," says Matt. "Perhaps, she has a secret account somewhere."

"Again the device that Bob knows about does the job and the remains are placed in the large storage container," adds Ashley.

"We know all of this is because we have communicated with one another," says Margaret. "But, how does the operation get started in the first place?"

"That's easy," says the General. "Some racketeer somewhere in the U.S., or from some foreign affiliation, approaches the women and sets it all up. It takes a large part of the profit, and scares the daylight out of her by saying she will be turned in to the authorities if she tells anyone.."

"Then when she gets too old for the job," adds Anna, "The operation just goes to sleep."

Bob was busy looking at his cell phone and added, "There are at least 10 adds targeting men over 40 who are looking for a partner, and they contain some pretty nice looking chicks."

"Lets have our English Treacle pudding and get back to it afterwards," said the General. "I see Matt over there looking at his satellite phone."

Matt had called Kimberly Scott the governmental information specialist who had a super computer at her disposal. Matt gave her the situation and asked if she had any information on it.

"Matt, this was the biggest secret problem in the country, last year. It has an enormous black budget line item in the President's budget last year. Each and every club – that's what they called them – is listed and the madam is identified. There was a enormous problem. Many football coaches, baseball players, congressmen, CEOs, and others is listed as clients. The political pressure was very high. They even had a team that went out to check them out by acting as customers. The team discovered that the whole operation was run by a European group hosted in of all places France. I was told to take the data out of the database but I didn't do it and just renamed it

Religious Items. The new President heard about it and did not know what to do. There was some killing of the johns involved and the government cleaned that up. Johns are the men that bought into the crimes and were killed. The leader of the U.S. government group told me it was building up again. He was sure they would start up with another kind of operation. The control group, the bad guys in this case, seek to in discredit the United States. He said things like this are all over the place. Sorry, there is no report on the latter subject."

Matt continued, "I received some information from Kimberly and I will summarize it after our tasty dessert."

CHAPTER 7

ON THE WAY HOME

On the way home after the dinner and meeting, Bob said nothing to Margaret, who was equally quiet. Finally, she said, "I wonder what is going to happen to Alan?"

"I liked him," said Bob. "Maybe he works for the U.S. Government, and when I did not see him, he was in training. He worked for NASA. I read they had 30,000 people working on the space program when they went to the moon. I wonder what they are all doing."

"I imagine that some are deceased, some living with their families, some still working on just about anything, some are still at NASA, and some are living with their girlfriend in a nice beachfront mansions," answered Margaret. "I would guess that many are proud of their work and just sitting back an enjoying life, drinking Carmel Machiattas with their spouses."

"I think many couples are pretty much like us with household tasks and helping each other out, and talking about things, and then making quilts with friends and playing golf, and going to entertainments of various kinds" replied Bob. "They aren't running about looking for special activities of who knows what form."

"People who have lost their spouse are lonesome," mumbled Margaret. "They want to say 'Hi. I'm home', 'How was your day', or 'Boy, I'm tired' to someone that cares. When something interesting happened, having someone to tell is important. Or, 'Do you want to hear what happened to Millie at the car dealer'? When something good or bad happens, you like to tell someone."

"I hope the General comes up with something," he seemed like a real general and his wife, what is her name 'Anna', seemed like a good team," said Bob. "I seem to feel, though, that Mat and Ashley are the big brains and he called someone in Washington right off. He seemed to ready to get started, and his wife Ashley was as quick as a whip."

"Do you like her more than me?" quipped Margaret. "She was beautiful."

"No, you know better than that," said Bob. "You will always be my best girl. She is beautiful. But she probably had two face jobs and speech training. You were beautiful right out of the box."

"You do not seem so interested in this problem – I should say situation," said Ashley. "You called Kimberly so quickly, as if to get it out of the way before it got started. You were tapping your paper with the pen as if to say 'get this boring stuff over with'. You are not usually that impatient. Was it the General? Was it that guy Bob?"

"It was the whole situation," answered Matt. "That was just one case, and it could be on the up-and-up. It probably is. But, in the whole realm of things, it is just peanuts. Also, there are people all over committing crimes against citizens. American people do it; French people do it; Chinese do it. Every time something happens, they blame it on Russian dissidents. I think we should just put it to sleep. If it just happens again, we should think about it."

"I agree," said Ashley. "Margaret and Bob are nice people, we were good to do what we did."

"Well, we did it," said the General. "I'm glad it's over. It's in Matt's hands now. There are a lot of problems in the world, except in this case. A problem doesn't exist. It's just an idea at this point."

"That gentleman Bob should be writing novels; he has a good imagination," said Anna. "He and Margaret are a nice couple. She was a good dresser. The thing I noticed about them is that they both had such good articulation. Their parents must have done a superb job of bringing them up. Also, their table manners were perfect."

"You should talk," smiled the General as he talked. "You are extremely good yourself in are respects."

CHAPTER 8

⟡◆◆◆⟡

NOT SO FAST LADIES AND GENTLEMEN

Alan was a happy man. He had a companion that was more pleasant than he could ever imagine. Daisy was the best. The meals were good, her speech was perfect, and she always seemed to bring up subjects he liked to converse about. She always awakened earlier than he in the morning and gave him a cheerful "Good Morning' with a big smile.

Daisy dressed well and made him proud when they were out to dinner and went to plays and musicals at the local theatre. Alan was a happy man, indeed. He hesitated giving his retirement money but felt that was his best investment he had made in his entire life.

It was late on a Saturday afternoon and Alan, a big sports fan, was watching a game in the living room. Daisy was out in the garage doing something.

"Alan," said Daisy. "Can you please come out and help me with something?"

"Sure," replied Alan as he headed for the garage.

Daisy was at the storage container. The door was open.

"It's in there," said Daisy.

Alan took two steps in the container, and Daisy smashed his head with a small hatchet. Daisy closed the door and went back inside the house after securing the door to the container. 'They will take care of him tomorrow," she thought. A little for them and a little for me. It's all in a day's work.

CHAPTER 9

MATT GETS THE BUG

Ashley awakened. It was 5:30 in the morning and Matt wasn't there. He had never done this before. Usually when he go up early, he was standing at the end of the bed with a steaming hot cup of delicious coffee. He knew exactly how to make it the way she liked it.

She walked down the hallway and there he was in his study working on something. It was math but she had no idea about what it was.

"Do you have a paper due?" asked Ashley. "I'll make you some coffee."

"It's this business with Bob and Margaret, and it seems to be stuck in my brain," said Matt. "Bob is an experienced professor and he seems to sense something. It is just like Clark always said that after 30 years in the Army as an officer, he could tell the what the soldier was going to say just by looking at him. It is the same with professors. I do it all the time. That's how I always have such a quick answer. Bob senses something in that relationship between his friend Alan and Daisy, but can't put it into words. I have the same feeling about Bob, himself."

"I know what you mean," said Ashley. "It's the same but different. Here's a stupid example what I am referring to. You ask a driver to pick up someone at the airport. The driver was out late last night with his girlfriend and is a bit tired so he stops for a cup of coffee. He's a little behind schedule, speeds it up, and gets a speeding ticket. Whose fault is it? Of course, it's the driver. But his lawyer says, you are at fault because he had to speed to make it on time to pick up the passenger. Probably, you know he will speed but never say a word about it. It's a little like Watergate, that pops up every election."

"Now, I get what you're thinking," replied Matt. "It's not only what the giver is thinking but also what the receiver is thinking. So in the case of Bob and Daisy, and the in-between person Alan, I have to figure out what is going on. Well, sweet person, that is exactly what I was trying to do using the combination of evidence using Dempster-Shafer Theory."

"Starbucks?" asked Matt. "You bet," was Ashley's answer.

CHAPTER 10

+◆◆◆◆+

THE HAIRCUT TO END ALL HAIRCUTS

"Do you think I need a haircut?" asked Bob. "It feels a little long around the ears."

"No, you don't need a haircut," said Margaret. "You're not fooling anyone. I'll make an appointment with Daisy. When do you want it?"

"Okay, let's say tomorrow," answered Bob. "I have an important meeting on that new missile and space system."

Margaret had a hard time stopping her laugh. Bob was retired.

So Margaret called Daisy and made an appointment for the next day. Daisy was busy but Margaret mentioned the Bob had an important meeting on the new missile and space system, and Daisy agreed to squeeze him in. Maybe someone would not show up, as was frequently the case with older women who had to get their girdles on, and had to make several tries. *Note: you are supposed to laugh here all you gentlemen.* The agreed upon time was 4:00 pm.

Bob arrived at 3:55 and there was a sign on the door that read, "Walk right in." Bob cautiously entered and there was Daisy who gave him a big American hug and pointed to the mud room hair salon.

Daisy sat down facing Bob and said, "He hit me."

"I'm sorry," said Bob. "Are you okay?"

"I had to pay him $300,000," replied Daisy.

Bob didn't know exactly what to say, so he eased out, "Was that his share of the house?"

Daisy nodded 'yes' and started cutting Bob's hair that wasn't that long to start with. Daisy was cheerful for a person who had been slugged twice: once from the guy and also hit with a bill of $300,000.

When the haircut was just about finished, Daisy said nicely, "Bob, tell me about that new project of yours on missiles and space."

Bob was on the spot but replied in a hurry, "We're in the formative stage and there is a potential problem with thrust boosters and also with a leak in the hydraulic system. In our penultimate meeting, several persons introduced items resulting from a conspecific study of the equipment." After years of teaching, Bob knew quite well how to kill a question session."

"Well, there you go Bob, a handsome as ever, " said Daisy as she finished the haircut.

Bob handed her a twenty from his wallet and said "Thanks, Daisy. Another good job."

Bob headed for the door expecting to see Alan at the counter. No Alan. No potato chips. No soft drink.

All Bob thought was that Alan was another victim of an unscrupulous woman.

———— ∞∞∞ ————

Margaret met Bob at the door, "You look good, young man."

All Bob said was, "She got Alan."

"I'm so sorry sweetie," said Margaret. "Just sit down and I'll get you a cup of coffee. I just made it for when you returned."

"She said 'he hit me' and that she had to pay him $300,000," blurted out Bob. "She did not pay him a cent. It's a con job. Now Matt, Ashley, and the General will believe me.

"Anna, too," added Margaret. "What happened to Alan?"

"I do not know," said Bob. "I can only think the worst."

✦✦✦✦✦

CHAPTER 11

THE TEAM IS BACK IN THE GAME

They agreed to again meet in the conference room in the Green Room restaurant. When the General was initially informed of the situation, he mentioned that his housekeeper was not yet cleared and that was the reason for the Green Room. He reminded Matt and Ashley that he felt this could end up being something in their ongoing agreement with the President and with Mark Clark, former four star General and currently Director of Intelligence, on the Deep Learning project.

"I don't know," said the General, "We have to pay high honorariums and then put up with irritating behavior. I wish Anna were here."

"Call her and just tell her about the new events and then kind of ease into what to pay them," said Ashley. "That Margaret runs the show, and I am sure we will get our moneys worth, but Bob, that's your area Matt."

"Bob is not as irritating as you guys think," added Matt. "He just saw through this operation right off. While you two are working out this ridiculous problem, I'll call Kimberly and see what they have on Daisy. Does anyone have any idea what Daisy's last name is. At least the name she is using."

"Ask Margaret," said Ashley.

"Okay, I'll wait," replied Matt.

When they got there, Margaret and Bob were sitting in the lobby. Margaret was happy to see them, as she was completely overloaded with comments from her worked-up husband. She was sympathetic, though, because Alan was not her friend, although she was friendly with him, but he was Bob's friend and they had spent many hours together discussing just about everything a person could think of. Bob smiled also, he was comfortable with Matt and the General.

Matt asked Margaret if she knew Daily's last name, and she looked in her cell phone. "It's Krolski,' said Margaret."

"Is that 'ski' or 'sky'?" asked Matt.

"I don't know," said Margaret. "I wrote 'ski'. She didn't spell it for me."

"It doesn't matter if she is American, but if she is not, then it gives us some information, possibly," answered Matt.

The General, Ashley, Margaret, and Bob went into the conference room while Matt went into the General's study and called Kimberly on his satellite phone.

"Hi Matt," said Kimberly. "Do you need information, or do you just want to talk?"

"I need information but I don't mind talking," said Matt. "Are you free right now?"

"I'm always free for you Matt," answered Kimberly, "But I was just looking at my cell phone."

"It's on the subject of rich women and their boyfriends," said Matt. "Just like we talked a couple of days ago. A case popped up that looks suspicious. Do you have anything on a Daisy Krolski?"

"Just a half second, The super computer is reorganizing the information," said Kimberly. "Okay, is that 'ski' or 'sky'?"

"Don't know," answered Matt.

"There is no 'ski' but there is a 'sky' in Florida," replied Kimberly. "Okay, hold on to your hat: She was a brain in school. Offered a Harvard scholarship but declined. Father owned and operated Daisy's Pizza. Brother killed in Viet Nam. She is okay with the IRS. Daisy worked in store. Old building on rented land. When father died, pizza parlor closed and land reused. Mother and Father deceased. Mother never worked. Daisy had hair dresser tranining but never practiced. Daisy died of Leukemia in 2010. Never married. And that's it."

"Any other Daisy Krolsky persons."

"No," said Kimberly. "Only she."

"Kimberly," said Matt. "You are a whiz."

"You can blame it on our super computer. I have a red light call. Call you back?"

"No and thanks."

Matt walked into the conference room and sat down. Everyone looked at him with anticipation.

All Matt said was, "We have a problem. It is a real problem."

CHAPTER 12

THEY REALLY DO HAVE PROBLEM

As Matt sat down, he said, "We have a tombstone person with whom to deal with, and they are the most trouble to deal with."

"What is a tombstone person?" asked Margaret.

"It's someone with a fake name taken off of a tombstone," said Bob.

"We can figure it all out," said Matt. "It's Krolsky not Krolski, so there is possibly a German connection, and in this morning's news, they said that the right wing dissidents in Germany are acting up again, and they are the Nazi symbolizers."

"Clark and the President should know about that supposition," said the General. "Even though we do not know anything more. I am going to take an honest risk, and Bob and Margaret should know about this. The team of Matt, Ashley, Anna, me, and a couple of others are involved with a possible problems that exists just below the surface. Little problems grow in size and Importance. There are line items on the President's budget that no one other than the top official of the President's office know about. We look for important things and bring them out in some form to the President and the Director of Intelligence. We just finished one on Artificial Intelligence. We get a large amount of money doing this and the reason it is high is the budget makers sometimes evaluate needs in different way. We, that is our government, uses zero based budgeting and that means that once an item gets on the budget it stays on the budget until someone takes it off. For example, as Ashley has pointed out, there are items for software for computers we no longer use. Companies take advantage of this and just continue to send the software to the parties that use the non-existent computers, President Jimmy Carter tried to eliminate zero-based budgeting but it didn't pass. We are on a project named *Deep Learning* with the objective of finding these hidden little unrecognized problems. Except, it is possible they will turn out to be important to the country. Deep Learning means digging deep to find those problems. The budget makers thought it is important, and it is, and gave it a reasonably high budget value. I administer this project for the country. I am hereby placing Robert and Margaret Anderson on the team. You are given an amount of money on a monthly basis to a bank account of your choosing. It is completely legal and totally tax free. Only you and the President, General Mark Clark, Director of Intelligence, and the team will know of this."

"You may use this money as you choose but it is not in your best interests to tell everyone," continued the General. "It will continue as long as the line in the President's budget exists, and that could be forever. The team consists of regulars and adjuncts. The regulars are given an honorarium of $1,000,000 per month and it is totally tax free. The adjuncts are called upon when needed and their amount is variable."

The General continued again, "If you agree to this, your position on the team starts immediately. The monetary aspect of this position seems a little high, but to our great nation, it is very important. Matt and Ashley can answer any questions you may have."

The General took a drink from a glass of water that Anna poured for him. He wasn't used to talking for such a long period on an important topic. He started up again, "The restaurant is now open for lunch, and we can pick up the meeting afterwards."

As the team left the conference room, the usual couple was sitting there watching. The woman said, "They look different today, like something has happened. The elderly woman is patting the arm of the elderly man. He must have done something good. The new couple look a little surprised, they are holding hands. The beautiful woman and the handsome tanned man are talking normally like it's another day at the bank." Her husband said, "To me, it looks like something very important has taken place. And it looks like the beautiful and handsome couple are the key elements. We have a fine country."

CHAPTER 13

- ◆ ◆ ◆ ◆ -

SORTING OUT THE PROBLEM
IF THERE IS ONE

Everyone came in and sat down where they were sitting before their fine luncheon. It looked differently with a medium-sized notebook, a gold fountain pen, small bottle of liquid ink, and a container of water with a fancy glass shaped like a U.S. government building.

Matt said, "When did this this happen?" and the General replied, "When Ashley went to the ladies room."

"He just wiggled his finger when we were eating and I caught the message," said Ashley. "I am surprised that you didn't pick it up Matt."

"I think I was too busy checking out the other diners," replied Matt with a big smile.

"How do we start?" asked the General.

"So, I guess we start with the U.S. government; it is always quick to jump into things," replied Ashley. "It has a lot of departments, but I don't know what they are."

"I do," said the General. I can list them; do you want me to?"

"Sure," said Matt. "I don't even have a clue about how many we have. Maybe 5."

"You will be totally surprised," answered the General. "Here I go, hold on to your hat:

Department of Agriculture
Department of Commerce
Department of Education
Department of Energy
Department of Health and Human Services
Department of Homeland Security
Department of Housing and Urban Development
Department of Interior
Department of Justice
Department of Labor
Department of State
Department of Transportation
Department of Treasury
Department of Veterans Affairs
Export-Import Bank of the United States – called EXIM
National Aeronautics and Space Administration
National Archives and Records Administration
National Institute of Standards and Technology
National Science Foundation
National Transportation Safety Board
Peace Corps
Small Business Administration
Social Security Administration
U.S. Agency for International Development
U.S. Environmental Protection Agency
U.S. General Services Administration
U.S. Office of Personnel Management

Whew."

"How many?" asked Matt with a smile on his face."

"Twenty-seven," answered the General. "Everyone knows that." He had a smile on his face.

"It's no wonder that you are a general," said Ashley.

"Remember we recommended the country should have an AI director for each agency to make sure they are using the best principles."

"And guidelines that they should follow," continued Matt. "That was a good start. Here is a short sentence that might serve as a good starting point: AI won't replace humans – but humans with AI will replace humans without AI. We could use a little AI on this project, but if and only if we really do have a problem and understand the AI. Margaret and Bob, AI stands for Artificial Intelligence."

"We know about AI Matt," interrupted Margaret. "Bob and I bought this book in the bookstore, and we kind of read it together. The Title is *Advanced Lessons in Artificial Intelligence: A Technical Novel and a Readable Primer*. In the first part there is dialogue as they are learning AI together and interacting. Then, there is a primer at the end for people who want to read about the subject and understand more about how it could be used. It has 541 pages and was published in this year 2024. You could read the primer first and then the lessons would be like an interesting novel. Our friends think we are experts. Would you like to borrow our copy?"

"I'm glad you are on the team," said the General.

"Kimberly said we could also contact one of the U.S. Intelligence Agencies," Matt. "General can you list all of them, also?"

"Sure," said the General. "Do you want me to list them also?"

"If you can Sir, but I really doubt it," said Matt. Still surprised over

the department list.

"Hold on to your hat again," said the General:

Defense Intelligence Agency
National Reconnaissance Office
Air Force Intelligence Surveillance and Reconnaissance Agency
Military Intelligence Corps
Coast Guard Intelligence
Department of Homeland Security
Marine Corps Intelligence
National Geospatial-Intelligence Agency
National Security Agency
Department of Energy
Drug Enforcement Administration
Bureau if Intelligence and Research
Department of the Treasury
Federal Bureau of Investigation
Office of Naval Intelligence
Office of the Director of National Intelligence
Department of State

United States Space Force
Advanced Technical Intelligence Center
National Space Intelligence Center
Central Intelligence Agency

And, the Director of National Intelligence is the principal adviser to the President."

"I'm more than impressed," said Matt. "We have to get this problem delineated before we contact anyone. Otherwise, we will make complete fools out of ourselves. I feel like a fool already."

"We have had enough for one day," said the General. "If you could make a plan for us Matt, we can get together either tomorrow or the next day."

"Let's meet again tomorrow," replied Margaret. "We have good momentum already."

"Okay said the General," said the General. "Can we meet again here tomorrow at just after the lunch crowd and I'll have the chef think of something difference for lunch.

CHAPTER 14

MATT MAKES A PLAN

Matt was not at all pleased on the way home, and Ashley was only a little better. They had driven more than half way before either of them said anything and it was Ashley.

"Did you like the way your grandfather was showing off by knowing all of those departments and agencies, and then to top it off, he planned all these lunches and had someone put out all of those meeting instruments?"

"He might have been showing off for Anna, and he should know by now that he couldn't fool her with all of those shenanigans," replied Matt with a smirk on his face. "I guess I should give it a good shot at making a plan, and maybe some good will come out of it."

"You'll do a good job of it; you always do," answered Ashley. "It could be that there is nothing to it."

"But wouldn't one of those intelligence agencies do a better job of it than we could do," replied Matt. "They are professionals at it with training and experience."

"I'll tell you what," said Ashley. "Why don't you just talk about a plan and I'll write it down while you are talking, and then we can refine it."

They got home, Ashley got a ton of 8 ½ X 11 pads and a handful of ball point pens and sat down at the dining room table. Matt stood up like a college professor, just as he was in everyday life.

Okay, professor, let's get going said Ashley with a smile on her face. Matt started:

Problem

We have a situation wherein a man, not necessary and elderly, man, moves in with a woman with an appropriate residence. Question. What can or will happen?

In general, there are two distinct possibilities: they are living together in a residence of moderate value and would like to upgrade. They are not married for a reasonable reason. They purchase a residence, with a value of $600,000. They each pay 50%. In the second possibility, the woman lives in a upper-class residence, say in the amount of $600,000. Man meets woman and she accepts him with a payment of $300,000. It could be recorded in a deed or not.

A typical example could be a woman with a former occupation of that of a hairdresser, through which she can meet men. It could be an widowed or divorced man with money.

They could have met through a cell phone ad by a woman intended for men over 40 years old, which is likely the case.

The man is congenial so that he could or would be noticed by other persons. Another characteristic is that the man has no family or other means of recognition if he is missing.

A Friend or customer visits the woman and is told "he hit me," and he is no longer there. Also, she has to pay him $300,000 for his share. There is no evidence if the man is alive or dead, received any money, and whether or not someone is notified. This is assumed to be the case.

The woman's working name is Daisy. Friend visits Daisy for service like a haircut, and notices a large compartment in the garage ostensible for a lawn mower or a motorcycle, or something.

Friend is asked to help Dawith something in the garage and sees that structure. Asks, and is told that where she puts bodies. No useful comments by Friend, and leaves without seeing a boyfriend.

Some time later, Friend visits Daisy for a haircut and notices the person from the breakfast club who he has befriended. He is surprised and acknowledges said acquaintance.

Friend thinks something is afoot and makes an excuse for a haircut for space technology meeting and receives the same "he hit me" exclamation and payment pf $300,000. He is again asked to Help Daisy and gets the same remark about bodies.

When leaving, Friend notices that the person from the breakfast club is not there. Friend is suspicious that a repetative is taking place and calls his associate from the university. He is Professor. They meet and a plan to test the scenario is conceptualized. Professor establishes the following scenario for solution to the problem, if there is one.

Solution

A policeman is contacted, Harry Steevens, is contacted to establish a group of police associates to visit women that advertise for male companions. A sample is developed through a government woman,

Kimberly Scott, who has results from previous investigations. Ten women are selected, and several policemen are selected to entertain the ladies. Each women is visited by two 'clients', one whose has relatives that would know he is missing and another who has no relatives. There is no evidence of foul play in any of the investigative cases. Daisy is alone in her behavior

Harry Steeves arranges to have a static drone employed to establish what is going out in Daisy's home. It is directed to an appropriate place and transmits images of the object in question. Her everyday behavior and extracurricular actives are noted and an undercover search of the facility is established. No bodies are found.

Friend is investigated and then the Director of National Intelligence is notified to assign the problem to one of the agencies. It is established that Friend is attempting to develop a methodology to establish money for one of the upcoming elections.

End of Plan

"Well, that is my first draft at a plan," said Matt.

"That is very good," replied Ashley. "Who is Friend."

"It is Bob, but I do not feel that his wife Margaret is also involved," answered Matt. "I do not think, so far, that he has committed a crime."

"So why is he doing it?" asked Ashley.

"What he wants to do is have the some outside group, like some right wing dissidents in Germany finance the election by running a string of people like Daisy. Bob is sponsored by the President but not directly. He just says to the people working for him that it would be fortunate if something like that happened, but he specifically did not say to do it. That worked the same way right down the line until they got to Bob, and he is the fall guy. Bob is trying to establish a cover for his illegal work, as in the previous Watergate Case that received public attention."

'Do you mean that the work that you and I, the General, Mark Clark, and the rest of the team is involved in this?" asked Ashley.

"That is precisely what I mean," said Matt.

"I think we should rest until our minds are clear," continued Ashley. Let's have a bowl of hot popcorn and watch a movie. We can postpone tomorrow's meeting. Wait!"

"Margaret," said both Matt and Ashley at the same time. "She wanted to move on it tomorrow."

CHAPTER 15

INTRODUCING THE ABSTRACT PLAN
TO THE PROVISIONAL TEAM

"You've been listening while I have been talking," said Matt to Ashley. "How should we proceed?"

"I think we should present the problem and a solution to the team, and not give the result as you have presented it," said Ashley. "Have the General call the 'case closed' and disband the team as far as Bob and Margaret are concerned. Terminate Bob and Margaret after one month's service, and put it to sleep as far as they are concerned and we are concerned."

"Not so fast," interrupted Matt. "We need to give Harry a chance to perform his end of the operation, and then kill the operation. At least as far as Bob and Margaret are concerned. Then have the Director of National Intelligence's team take over following Bob and Margaret. Hopefully, by then it will be out of our hands. However, Bob and Margaret will know that we are checking out the madams and they perhaps will put the madams on the alert. Maybe! Then the selected agency will have to decide whether to work with Harry Steevens or use their own methodology and personnel."

"Another possibility is that the director's team would prefer to work through us to interface with Bob and Margaret," added Ashley.

"I just thought of another thing," continued Matt. Perhaps our President is running that show to obtain money to work against his competitor. It will be against the enemy, that is the political opponent. It could be totally negative and assume that it is stuff that would be unpopular for a sitting President to do. If it were in the Presidential budget then the courts could take a look at it. Just a thought, but something like that."

"Let's put it all together and present it at tomorrow's meeting, and then take it from there," said Ashley. "We will rehash this subject a million times – but you know what I mean. Let me type this and then hang it up for the day."

"Good job Sweetie," said Matt.

"You've never said that before. It sounds quite good."

The report for the provisional team starts here.

Scenario of the Problem

A potential problem situation where a man moves in with a woman with an everyday residence. They like each other, perhaps even love each other. We are interested in what can happen next.

In general, there are two distinct possibilities: they are living together in a residence of moderate value and would like to upgrade. They are not married for a reasonable reason, such as the woman is receiving alimony. They purchase a residence, with a value of $600,000. This is just a nominal number for illustration only. They each pay 50%.

In the second possibility, the woman lives in a upper-class residence, say in the amount of $600,000. Man meets woman and she accepts him with a payment of $300,000. It could be recorded in a deed or not.

A typical example could be a woman with a former occupation of that of a hairdresser, through which she can meet men. It could be a widowed or divorced man with money.

They could have met through a cell phone ad by a woman intended for men over 40 years old, which is likely the case. A typical characteristic is that the man has no family or other means of recognition if he is missing.

A Friend or customer visits the woman and is told "he hit me," and he is no longer there. Also, she has to pay him $300,000 for his share. There is no evidence if the man is alive or dead, received any money, and whether or not someone is notified. This is assumed to be the case.

The woman's working name is Daisy. Friend visits Daisy for service like a haircut, and notices a large compartment in the garage ostensible for a lawn mower or a motorcycle, or something.

Friend is asked to help Daisy with something in the garage and sees that structure. Asks, and is told that where she puts bodies. No useful comments by Friend, and leaves without seeing a boyfriend. The worst 'bodies' is an operant word here.

Some time later, Friend visits Daisy for a haircut and notices the person from the breakfast club who he has befriended. He is surprised and acknowledges said acquaintance. Friend is retired.

Friend thinks something is afoot and makes an additional excuse for a haircut for space technology meeting and receives the same "he hit me"

61

exclamation and payment pf $300,000. He is again asked to Help Daisy and gets the same remark about bodies.

When leaving, Friend notices that the person from the breakfast club is not there. Friend is suspicious that a repetative action is taking place and calls his associate from the university. He is Professor. They meet and a plan to test the scenario is conceptualized. Professor establishes the following scenario for solution to the problem, if there is one..

Planned Solution

A policeman is contacted, known as Police, is contacted to establish a group of police associates to visit women that advertise for male companions. A sample is developed through a government woman, named Super, who has results from previous investigations. Ten women are selected, and several policemen are selected to entertain the ladies. Each women is visited by two 'clients', one whose has relatives that would know he is missing and another who has no relatives.

Police will also arranges to have a static drone employed to establish what is going out in Daisy's home. It will be directed to an appropriate place in order to transmits image of the object in question. To determine everyday behavior and extracurricular activity an undercover search of the facility is planned.

The team of then General, Anna, Matt, Ashley, Bob, and Margaret meet in the Green Room conference room and Ashley presents the problem and solution. Everyone is unusually somber.

When the typed version is handed out, not a person says a word. The General mentioned that Police needs time to investigate the situation and that he will call a meeting in 4 or 5 weeks.

The General adjourns the meeting and they all head for the eating area. A light lunch of cob salad and French bread is served and a slice of pound cake with coffee is served as desert. Things perked up a bit, but it seemed like no one cared anyone cared about the case of Daisy and her boyfriends.

Matt and the general headed for the golf course. Ashley and Anna headed for the expensive hair dresser and manicurist. Bob and Margaret headed home.

CHAPTER 16

+ ◆ ◆ ◆ ◆ +

THE WORST ROUND OF GOLF EVER

The round of golf started out poorly. They had to wait because there was a women's tournament going on and tee time was a problem. Then to top it off, on the first tee, Matt took a 3 wood out of bag instead of his driver and got a poor start. Then, believe it or not, the General did the same dumb thing.

"It's that Daisy problem," said Matt. "It's got us both rattled."

"You're right there," said the General. "I can't get the whole thing off my mind. There is something going on and I don't like it. Let's put this problem aside and enjoy our round of golf; we can pick it up again when we have our usual pick-me-up when we are finished. No talking about it at the ninth hole, and you are the major instigator of talking then."

"Okay, okay," said Matt,

True to form, Matt started the discussion again at the ninth hole. "Do you remember the name of that friend Ashley had in South Carolina. They had some quilting club that they called the Fab Five. I wonder if she has any knowledge of the women who lure in men to their domain?"

"Maya Wilson," said the General.

"You sure have some memory," answered Matt. "First you remember the departments and agencies in the government and now you remember the name of a person you probably only saw once."

"Comes with age," quipped the General with a big smile.

"She might have some insight into these things, oh, I already said that," said Matt. "I'll have to ask Ashley."

"That's a good idea," said the General, "There are plenty of older women in South Carolina and Sun City. A person never knows beforehand where you get information. You feel going down for a golfing visit."

"We have to arrange with Harry Steevens and that is where he might be working these days. He loves this undercover stuff."

"Let's get going with this golf," replied the General. "It might be starting to drizzle."

"South Carolina seems like a good idea to me," said Matt as they headed off the course. We will have to arrange with Harry Steevens to somehow take time off from his normal duties, if he wants to, and round up other people, not necessary policeman, to check out the women that Kimberly selects for us."

"This is going to take some careful planning, don't you think?" asks the General.

CHAPTER 17

✦✦✦✦✦

THE NINETEENTH HOLE

"That was the worst 18 holes that I have ever played," said the General as they headed toward the clubhouse. "How about you Matt?"

"Same with me," responded Matt. "As I said before, it probably is that Daisy project – to use the name that doesn't mean anything; to me anyway. It's not the project per se, but the fact that we are involved with it. Undoubtedly, it will help someone, but at this moment, I don't know exactly who that could be."

"What are you drinking," asked the General.

"I'm going to try that new non-alcoholic beer with only 50 calories per bottle. The name is Zero."

"Must be an AI name," answered the General. "I'm going to have a single malt scotch over ice. Zero beverage that has 50 calories. Sound like AI, and they think it's going to takeover the world."

"I think, I'll have a cheeseburger also," replied Matt. "I've been a little hungry lately."

"I'll do the same," said the General. "That new housekeeper is a new kind of cook and I haven't been eating much lately. Want a filet and your favorite loaded baked potato for dinner this evening? I know Anna and Ashley definitely wouldn't mind."

"Sounds good, but I'm still having the burger."

"Did your father drink alcoholic beverages; I don't know why I'm asking," said the General. I should know, he's my son, but for the life in me, I don't know it."

"I don't think he does," answered Matt. "Neither does my mother. We always had beer in the fridge and whiskey above the fridge in the cabinet. We had visitors – usually on Sundays – and they served it. I never saw them drink alcoholic beverages. At dinner, they had coffee and we – the kids – had milk. If we· got thirsty, we drank milk then also. My lifelong buddy down the street asked his father of he could smoke and his father gave him a cigarette and he didn't like it. Same with beer. I asked my father if I could try beer and he said 'There is some in the fridge, try it.' I tried it and the result was the same as with my friend's cigarette. My father and mother were strict, probably learned it from you. My father came home the same time every day and the meal was the same every day. We always had meat, starch, like potatoes, salad, veggies, bread, and dessert. Every day, except on vacation that we took every year, and Saturdays and Sundays. I think we are trying to avoid the main subject, which is this Daisey problem."

"What about Harry Steevens?" asked the General

"We are going to have to work out how many women will be involved, and how many police people will be needed. They don't necessarily have to be police but if this goes to court sometime, that could be significant. Each woman will receive two visitors: one with normal friends and family, and the other which no discernable friends, family, or anyone. We should visit each woman only twice, else they will get wise that something is going on. Also, you can't have two exclusive police for each women, that would entail the whole police force. The perps will see through it right away."

"But I have a thought," continued Matt. "You know that Ashley and I kind of suspect Bob and Margaret. For sure Bob, and probably Margaret. They would warn the women."

"You have a solution?" asked the General.

"Indeed I do," said Matt. "When we have our next meeting, Have Harry say that he could not find any way to find enough policemen to do the job. So that aspect of the job is finished and cancel the project."

Matt continued. "In secret, Harry should pursue the plan and report only to you, Ashley, Anna, and me. Also, Harry should us a static drone on Daisy and determine when we can look in the compartment I the garage. Here is what I think, Daisy did not kill anyone, and the project to make money for some German right wing people is just getting started. There is plenty of time before the next election. As far as the government is concerned, neither Bob nor Margaret has done anything illegal. We turn the project over to the Director of National Intelligence. Subsequently, the Director of National Intelligence may request the team of you, Ashley, Anna, and me to take over."

"Is that it?" asked the General.

"I believe so," replied Matt. "Harry will do the original plan, and if it is as we suspected, then turn that information over to the Director.

CHAPTER 18

THE PROJECT IS ENDED

Harry Steevens announced to the team in a regularly scheduled meeting that he could not pull together enough men to do the investigative job as planned. Bob and Margaret were notified that they would be awarded one months honorarium and their contribution was no longer necessary. What ever went on between them is not known by the General and they were to assured that their slate was clean and they could go in whatever direction with the conceptual problem, as they wished. Both were overjoyed and seemed relieved to have it done with. The General was pleased that the outsiders were out of the picture.

Harry convinced the chief of police that a government sponsored investigated was under way and it would involve at least 10 men from the force to investigate the sample of 10 'rich' women who had advertised for older male companionship. The reason for the men's contribution was clearly indicated. Their methodology was their own personal business, and their own police work would not be affected. They had to sign a government document and were promised a million dollar tax free honorarium. The project was U.S. Government top secret, not to be mentioned to anyone. The manner they were selected and how they did their assignment was not indicated. Only unmarried men were selected and their behavior was indeed influenced by the situation that previously existed with Daisy.

Harry arranged for the static drone to be used and Daisy's secret compartment in her garage turned out to be not of concern. It was only lawn equipment. Daisy was a bit of a joker.

There was only one remaining task. The President, the Director of Intelligence Clark, and the National Director of Intelligence ha to be contacted.

CHAPTER 19

NOT YET

Matt and the General were at the ninth hole and stopped for a breather. Did you ever wonder about why Matt and the General always seemed to start a conversation there? That's where the bathrooms are. Okay, the golf course has eighteen holes and its half way.

"You haven't mentioned that Daisy project, lately," said the General.

"Would you like for me to contact Harry Steevens, and start another one of those definitive efforts?" responded Matt.

"Clark called and there was something in the news about someone that got swindled," said the General. "I just thought of it."

"Maybe we should change it a bit," said Matt. "Perhaps our sample size was too small and maybe things have changed in the world of swindling people. Just change the project by lowering the price and perhaps only kicking the johns out and not killing them."

"What's this *johns* business?"

"That's the party that gets swindled," answered Matt.

"We could change the whole project and start an answering service or web site to record swindles, but doing it without recording names, or do both. We could stop that source completely." Said the General.

"Why not have the Department of National Intelligence or one of its agencies do it completely?" asked Matt.

"I think the reason is that they do not have a clean case against the people running the operation." Answered the General. "If they don't have a clear victory in easy sight, they are not interested."

"I think that is our job," said Matt. "We simply have to show how it is done. We know that already. I can write it up and then we go to Clark and the President. We need Harry Steevens and Kimberly Scott. We need to show that the money is going to illegally fund the opponents campaign for the White House. We need definitive information. Give me a couple of days and Ashley's assistance and we can complete a plan for approaching the situation. It's not a problem yet, but I guarantee you it will become one. We are smarter than they are and we can do it, if we work together."

CHAPTER 20

◆◆◆◆◆

MATT'S NEW PLAN TO GET THE BAD GUYS

It only took two large bowls of hot pop corn and two movies with in between thinking and writing, Matt and Ashley finished the project plan without a name. Even though working on it was miserable, both were a little sad that it soon would be over. They classed it Code Red Top Secret to insure to the recipients that it might be important.

Code Red Top Secret

The only eyes that should read this document are:

The President of the United States
The Director of Intelligence
The Director of National Intelligence

Source:

Dr. Matthew Miller
Gen Dr. Les Miller
Prof Ashley Miller

Outside personnel:

Mr. Harry Steevens
Ms. Kimberly Scott

Introduction

There is serious evidence that a right wing Nazi party in Germany has intentions to influence the presidential election to be executed in January 2025.

The funds for such influence are intended to be directed to the National Headquarters of said political party and disbursed in the generally accepted method supporting activities, travel, and planned events. It is estimated that the amount of such funds to be substantial. The methods and execution of such behavior is illegal by the Constitution of the United States. (Source: *The Constitution of the United States of America and other Classic American Documents,* New York: Fall River Press, 2017.)

Source of the Funds for Dispersal

A quick study on a cell phone and various computers is that there is usually shown on a given day several ads run to attract men over 40+ years for a nice looking woman for a male companionship. The statement of the ads reflects a companionship but in reality that is only assumed. The duration is only implied. So the relationship may be only for one date, but reflecting a longer period.

Below the surface, the women are looking for men with money to spend. Often the engagement is for a pleasant evening at an expensive restaurant. Sometimes the relationship is longer until it runs sour.

Frequently, the women are looking for a life in relationship in varying degrees that are tentatively forever, with the women and men sharing their wealth.

In the latter case, there are generally different situations. In the first case, the couple meet and agree to live together in a modest relationship. Then, they agree to buy an expensive home with joint ownership. Okay, so far. That is not against the law in any way, shape, or form. Then after reasonable time the relationship is ended for some reason and the man leaves and the women pays him for his share; she becomes the full owner. So now is the key point. The couple separates for some reason, like the men meets another woman, or she meets a more interesting man, or they wind up not liking each other. Not commonplace but certainly valid. She pays him his share and she is the full owner. If he has relatives, they know what is going on and establish reasonable settlement. But, if he has none, the options are endless. She just doesn't pay or he just runs off or he dies or is killed. The plot thickens.

If he is killed, the killer disposes of the body, and she has paid him no money. She meets another man with similar attributes and the process continues. She can have a sponsor with whom her shares the profit – legal or illegal. Persons that we know, believe that is the case and through our investigation, the resultant money in whole or in part is used for political reasons. The Names of the persons are Robert and Margaret Anderson, husband and wife.

Foreign Intervention

If it is the case that an outside agency, like a criminal enterprise or a foreign group that backs the operation and in some manner achieves the ownership for the woman, it is likely that is done for a reason, and in that case they probably expect a majority of the profits. When the woman stops providing profit then the operation then ceases to operate for that woman.

Analysis

A method for investigating and analyzing the above scenario has been achieved through the previously assigned project with the group known as Matt, Ashley, and the General. Under that realm and jurisdiction, a team formed from police officers and Kimberly Scott, an officer in the national jurisdiction have determined that the above scenario is indeed true and exists in various forms. In light of the forthcoming election, we have proof that the process is sponsored by the aforementioned organization exist in the form specified. We do not have proof that the funds go illegally to the political party.

Conclusion

The conclusion of the aforementioned team is the Director of National Intelligence through its member agencies do in fact the verify the assumed operation.

Disclaimer

This is a working document and be regarded as such.

CHAPTER 21

THE FINAL RESULT

The selected National Intelligence team operating under code red top secret with the code name *z-team* without the specific request of the President and the Director of National Security investigated the aforestated class of incidents and determined that the outside funds if accepted by the political team would be classified as a crime against the United States of America. The funds were thereby not accepted by the political party.

Key testimonial was given by Robert and Margaret Anderson and were classed as heroes by the journalistic press.

Prior to the election of 2025, a large trial took place and the foreign entities were exposed and duly admonished.

CHAPTER 22

✦✦✦✦✦

A LOOK AT WATERGATE

From ChatGPT
(September 17, 2024)

Watergate refers to a political scandal in the United States in the early 1970s that ultimately led to the resignation of President Richard Nixon. It began with a break-in at the Democratic National Committee headquarters, located in the Watergate office complex in Washington, D.C., on June 17, 1972.

The burglars were attempting to wiretap phones and steal documents, and it was later revealed that they were connected to Nixon's re-election campaign.The scandal grew when it was discovered that members of Nixon's administration were involved in efforts to cover up the break-in. Investigative journalism, especially by reporters Bob Woodward and Carl Bernstein, along with congressional hearings, uncovered widespread abuses of power by the Nixon administration, including illegal wiretapping, political sabotage, and obstruction of justice.

A crucial part of the scandal was the revelation that Nixon had secretly recorded conversations in the White House. These tapes provided evidence that Nixon had participated in the cover-up of the Watergate break-in. Facing near-certain impeachment, Nixon became the first U.S. president to resign from office on August 8, 1974.

Watergate had a lasting impact on American politics, leading to reforms designed to increasansparency in government and a general decline in public trust in political institutions.

From Copilot
(September 17, 2024)

The Watergate scandal was a major political controversy in the United States during the early 1970s. It began with a break-in at the Democratic National Committee headquarters at the Watergate complex in Washington, D.C., on June 17, 1972. The burglars were connected to President Richard Nixon's re-election campaign, and they were caught wiretapping phones and stealing documents1.

The scandal escalated as it was revealed that high-ranking officials in Nixon's administration were involved in the cover-up of the break-in. Investigative journalists Bob Woodward and Carl Bernstein of The Washington Post played a crucial role in uncovering the details, with the help of a secret informant known as "Deep Throat"1.

As the investigation progressed, it was discovered that Nixon had secretly recorded conversations in the Oval Office. These tapes provided evidence of his involvement in the cover-up. Facing imminent impeachment, Nixon resigned from the presidency on August 9, 1974.

The Watergate scandal had a profound impact on American politics, leading to greaterscrutiny of political leaders and reforms aimed at increasing transparency and accountability in government

ABOUT THIS BOOK

The story described herein has been developed to entertain the reader. The plot is only imagined and probably never occurred before. But you never know. Stranger things have happened. Who would imagine that Watergate would have happened from more simpler events.

The book is easy reading and is not a contribution to literature. It does not present violence, sex, or bad language. It is accessible by practically any reader. There are plenty of opportunities, however, as is the case with almost any modern story.

A professional writer could do wonders with the story, as there are a lot of open items. This is by design. The lead time to make a movie would be incredibly short and that is a thing that should be considered. In fact, almost any actor could ad lib the verbal part without due consideration.

The idea of the story and conceptualization of a real life example would be a good subject to throw around and laugh at in any breakfast or Romeo club.

So, enjoy the read. It is short and be readable on the way home on the train or aircraft. One more thing, If you are an aspiring play or movie writer, this is a chance that will probably pass by again.

The Author
September, 2024

ABOUT THE AUTHOR

Harry Katzan, Jr. is a professor who has written several books and many papers on computers and service science. He has been an advisor to the executive board of a major bank and a general consultant on various disciplines. He and his wife have lived in Switzerland where he was a banking consultant and a visiting professor of Artificial Intelligence. He is an avid runner and has completed 94 marathons including Boston 13 times and New York 14 times. He holds bachelors, masters, and doctorate degrees.

RELATED BOOKS BY HARRY KATZAN JR.

Advanced Lessons for Artificial Intelligence

Conspectus of Artificial Intelligence

Artificial Intelligence is a Service

The K-REPORT

Strategy and AI

The Money Gate

Printed in the United States
by Baker & Taylor Publisher Services

Printed in the United States
by Baker & Taylor Publisher Services